Josh's Halloween Pumpkin

Josh's Halloween Pumpkin

By Kathryn Lay
Illustrated by Katy Bratun

PELICAN PUBLISHING COMPANY
GRETNA 2008

To my mom, Gladys Petrey, who always had a smiling face and now smiles at me down from Heaven. Thanks for always believing in my dreams.
—K. L.

*The word "Pelican" and the depiction of a pelican
are trademarks of Pelican Publishing Company, Inc.,
and are registered in the U.S. Patent and Trademark Office.*

Library of Congress Cataloging-in-Publication Data

Lay, Kathryn.
  Josh's Halloween pumpkin / by Kathryn Lay ; illustrated by Katy Bratun.
      p. cm.
  Summary: Josh learns a lesson about selfishness when he discovers an enormous pumpkin in his grandfather's pumpkin patch and his little sister goes missing.
   ISBN 978-1-58980-595-8 (hardcover : alk. paper) [1. Pumpkin--Fiction. 2. Selfishness--Fiction.] I. Bratun, Katy, ill. II. Title.
   PZ7.L445Jo 2008
   [E]--dc22

                              2008006324

Printed in Korea
Published by Pelican Publishing Company, Inc.
1000 Burmaster Street, Gretna, Louisiana 70053

JOSH'S HALLOWEEN PUMPKIN

As far as Josh could see, Grandpa Frank's pumpkin patch stretched in front of him, waiting for a game of hide-and-seek. The orange globes glowed under the full moon.

"Close your eyes and count to ten," he told Callie.

His little sister giggled. "One, two, six, eight . . ."

Josh stepped into the patch. He'd waited for the end of the long summer days and for October to come. The pumpkins were ready.

Josh dodged and weaved, careful not to get too far ahead of Callie as he traveled deeper into the patch. Just four, she was afraid of the dark—but never afraid of the pumpkins.

Then he was standing in front of the biggest pumpkin he'd ever seen.

Callie bumped into him and shouted, "You're it!"

Josh pulled her in front of the amazing pumpkin. "Big! Big punkin!" she shouted as she ran around and around it until Josh was dizzy.

He tried to wrap his arms around the pumpkin. "It's as big as the wheels on Grandpa's tractor."

He grabbed the thick stem and hopped up, pulling Callie to sit behind him. He imagined carving out the pumpkin—making windows and a door. "This is mine," he whispered. "My magic pumpkin. Grandpa just can't sell it."

Callie shouted, "Mine too!"

As he thought about all the things he could do with his giant find, Josh told her stories of smiling, winged pumpkins that gave rides to the bravest in the land.

The next morning, Grandpa Frank heaped waffles onto Josh's plate. "I'm expecting lots of customers this year."

"Coming to see the magic punkin!" Callie said.

Josh put a finger to his lips and winked at her. She winked back with both eyes. Grandpa Frank said she was so sweet that everyone bought their pumpkins just for a smile from her.

Josh ran outside at the *beep-beep* of a car horn. Mr. Biggs, the town barber, was their first customer every year. "Got your wagon ready?"

Josh nodded.

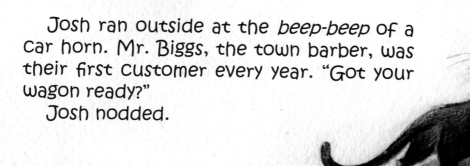

Big Bill, Grandpa's farm hand, loaned Josh
his pocketknife to cut the stems. Josh cut
each pumpkin from its vine as people came
from all around the county. He ran back
and forth, his wagon filled with pumpkins of
all sizes.

But the special pumpkin stayed hidden for
two days. Josh never took a customer near
it. He wondered how Grandpa had missed
something so big and full of possibilities.

On the third day, Mr. Keegan, the postman, discovered the pumpkin Josh had claimed as his own.

"Yes sirree, that's the biggest one I've ever seen," Mr. Keegan said.

Josh stood in front of the pumpkin. "It's not for sale."

"Not for sale?" Mr. Keegan repeated. "Fiddlesticks. Tell your grandpa I'll be back tomorrow and I'll pay him twenty-five dollars for it."

Josh slumped against his wagon. "You're mine," he told the pumpkin.

At the end of the day, when Grandpa took Callie to buy her dress for the Harvest Festival, Josh slipped into the quiet pumpkin patch. He took Big Bill's knife and sawed and sawed until the pumpkin fell from the vine.

He would be crowned the Harvest Festival Pumpkin King with such a thing, and he would ride in the biggest float of the parade.

Josh pushed and rolled the pumpkin until he found a hiding spot. Inside the barn. In a dark corner. Behind two bales of hay. And under an old quilt.

He jumped when Grandpa Frank burst into the barn and shouted, "Josh, come quick! Callie is missing somewhere in Fielder's Woods. We stopped at Joe Tyler's to see his new pups and she wandered away."

Josh's heart pounded. Callie was alone in the woods, the dark woods.

Grandpa Frank called Big Bill. "We need more help to search."

Josh remembered how Callie giggled and clapped as she listened to his stories about the pumpkin. "Wait, Grandpa. I've got an idea."

He walked to the dark corner of the barn, behind the bales of hay, and pulled the quilt from the pumpkin.

"How did that get in here?" Grandpa asked.

Josh explained his idea. Big Bill smiled.

Grandpa pointed at his field hand. "Call everyone in town. Tell them to bring their jack-o'-lanterns to Eagle Hill. Tell them Callie's missing. They'll come."

Josh and Grandpa Frank tied the pumpkin inside the wagon and pulled it to the bottom of Eagle Hill. They pulled and pushed and tugged the wagon until they reached the top, high above Fielder's Woods.

Josh watched as Grandpa cut around the stem of the pumpkin. Together they scooped out the mushy insides. Then Josh carved the pumpkin—two big round eyes, a huge triangle nose, and a wide smile. Inside, they set three tall candles.

"There," Grandpa Frank said.

They pulled the wagon with the huge jack-o'-lantern to the edge of the hill, on top of Lookout Rock.

Grandpa lit the candles and the pumpkin glowed.
"Do you think she'll see it?" Josh whispered.
Grandpa nodded. "It's as bright as the moon."
The wind whispered through the trees. Then, from the darkness, dozens of glowing faces appeared.
"Look!" Josh cried.
The townspeople walked across the field, carrying small jack-o'-lanterns. They placed them in two rows, making a path that led to Josh's secret pumpkin.

The crowd on Eagle Hill stood in silence and waited. Josh sat beside the pumpkin. The pumpkin smiled and Josh felt its magic.

Then, a noise. Just a tiny noise. Josh peered through the darkness, down the hill, and to the edge of the woods. A small figure walked toward them, slowly, up the hill. Then, that someone ran through the jack-o'-lantern path. Grandpa Frank stepped from the crowd as Callie leapt into his arms. The townspeople cheered.

Callie squirmed from Grandpa's hold and danced around the glowing jack-o'-lanterns. "Punkins! Pretty punkins!" She stopped in front of the biggest pumpkin and looked at Josh. "The magic punkin smiled at me in the dark. Was I brave?"

Josh hugged his sister. "You were brave."

Then they were surrounded as everyone hugged Callie and patted Josh's pumpkin. Callie gave a big yawn as the people gathered their pumpkins and walked down the hill to town. Josh watched the procession of glowing jack-o'-lanterns.

He sat in the cool grass and drew his legs up to his chin. Grandpa Frank settled beside him. They watched Callie talk to the pumpkin.

"That's some pumpkin," Josh said.

Grandpa smiled. "It sure is."

They sat side by side until the candles burned low inside the pumpkin. When the jack-o'-lantern face was dark and Callie yawned again, they tied the pumpkin to the wagon and walked home. Callie held tightly to Josh's hand.

"It's yours," Grandpa said, nodding toward the pumpkin.

Josh patted the bumpy skin and squeezed Callie's hand. "I know just what to do with it."

On the day of the Harvest Festival, Grandpa Frank drove the tractor that pulled the biggest float in the parade. The jack-o'-lantern smiled from the center of the float.

Callie, the Pumpkin Queen, rode the magic pumpkin as if they were flying through town. She waved and smiled to the people lining the street.

Josh stood beside Callie as she rode her winged pumpkin and whispered in her ear, "You really are the bravest in the land."